THE ZACK FILES™

I'm Out of My Body.... Please Leave a Message

By Dan Greenburg

Illustrated by Jack E. Davis

GROSSET & DUNLAP • NEW YORK

I'd like to thank my editors,
Jane O'Connor and Judy Donnelly,
who make the process of writing and revising
so much fun, and without whom
these books would not exist.

I also want to thank
Jennifer Dussling and Laura Driscoll
for their terrific ideas.

Text copyright © 1997 by Dan Greenburg. Illustrations copyright © 1997 by Jack E. Davis. All rights reserved. Published by Grosset & Dunlap, Inc., which is a member of The Putnam & Grosset Group, New York. THE ZACK FILES is a trademark of The Putnam & Grosset Group. GROSSET & DUNLAP is a trademark of Grosset & Dunlap, Inc. Published simultaneously in Canada. Printed in the U.S.A.

Library of Congress Cataloging-in-Publication Data

Greenburg, Dan.
    I'm out of my body—please leave a message / by Dan Greenburg ; illustrated by Jack E. Davis.
       p.   cm. — (The Zack files)
    Summary: When his friend Spencer, the class genius, spends the night, he and Zack discover how to leave their bodies and travel around New York City, but they have one problem—how to get back inside themselves.
    [1. Astral projection—Fiction.]   I. Davis, Jack E., ill. II. Title. III. Series: Greenburg, Dan. Zack files.
PZ7.G8278Im 1997
[Fic]—dc20   96-38190
                                                    CIP
                                                      AC

ISBN   0-448-41339-6 (pbk.)   C D E F G H I J

Chapter 1

"**Z**ack, have you ever been outside of your body?"

That's what my friend Spencer asked me. He was sleeping over at my house. It was a pretty weird question. But I happen to know a lot about weird.

My great-grandpa died, and came back as a cat. A ghost named Wanda trashed our apartment. Once I got an electric shock in science class, and I could read minds for a while. Oh, and there's a parallel universe on the other side of the medicine cabinet in my bathroom. As I say, I know a lot about weird.

Anyway, this out-of-body stuff was new to me. But it sounded kind of cool. My friend Spencer Sharp is the smartest kid in our class. Everybody knows it, including Spencer. I don't mean that the way it sounds. Spencer is very nice. And he's always up for trying something new. But I couldn't believe he knew something about weird stuff I didn't.

"How would you know if you were outside your body?" I asked him.

"Well, you'd be floating in the air and looking down at yourself," he said.

"But if my eyes were in my body, what would I be looking down at it *with*?" I asked.

"With the eyes in your *astral* body," he said.

"And what, exactly, is an astral body?" I asked.

"It's the one inside your regular one. The one you can travel out-of-body with."

We were sitting on the floor in my bedroom, leaning up against my brand-new bunk bed.

"How come you know about this stuff?" I asked.

Spencer pulled an old book out of his backpack and showed it to me. *Astral Travel for Beginners: Out-of-Body Journeys Through the World Mind.*

"I bought it at a used-book store," said Spencer. New York City has loads of used-book stores. And I bet Spencer has been in every one of them. "This book is from the

1960s," he said. "The hippie days. It looks great."

"What's so great about traveling out-of-body?"

"Well, it's faster than a plane. It's a whole lot cheaper. You don't have to stand in line to go through that stupid metal detector. And you never lose your bags. What do you say we try it tonight?"

Just then my dad came into my room. My mom and dad are divorced. I stay with each of them about half the time.

"Hey, guys," he said, "it's getting late. I know tonight's a Saturday. But I think it's time for bed. If you hurry, I'll let you talk in the dark for half an hour."

"OK," I said.

"Oh, I almost forgot," Dad said. "I just saw a mouse in the kitchen. So if you go in

~ 4 ~

there for a snack, you may have company."

Dad left, and Spencer and I got into our pajamas. Then we climbed into bed. He got the top bunk because he was the guest. That's really why Dad got me the bunk bed —for sleepovers.

"So what do you say, Zack?" asked Spencer after we turned off the lights. "You want to try some out-of-body travel tonight?"

"I don't know," I said. "I guess so."

He turned on his flashlight and opened his out-of-body book. He began to read aloud: "Get set for a groovy time. First, lie down with your eyes closed. Listen to wind chimes, if you have them. Be at one with the universe. Then place your left hand over your forehead. Right in the middle. Aquarian Age people call this the third eye. Then place your right hand over your belly button...."

"It actually says belly button?"

"It says navel, OK? I wasn't sure you knew the word."

Spencer doesn't usually act superior. But I hate it when he does. "Thanks for inter-preting," I said.

"Now let your astral body slowly seep out of your real one...through your *navel*. OK?" Spencer shot me a look. Then he went on reading. "Seep out and float above you like smoke...."

I tried doing what the book said. It didn't seem to be working.

"Are you doing all this too?" I asked.

"Of course," said Spencer. Spencer loves to say "of course."

"And is it working for you?" I asked.

"I don't know yet," he said.

That meant no. "Just keep trying," he said. "Sometimes it takes a while. Especially the first time."

"Have you done this a whole lot?" I asked.

"No, not that much."

"More than once?"

"Uh, no. Less."

We tried it for about an hour. Nothing happened. I told Spencer he must not be giving me the right directions. He said I must not be following them right. But nothing was happening to him, either.

And then, finally, I felt something. A little tickle against the hand on my belly button. "Seep out....Seep out," I kept telling my astral body.

A few minutes later I felt another tickle

against my hand. This time it was like a breath. I opened my eyes. I was almost out of my body! But my leg was stuck. It felt like I was in quicksand. I pulled and pulled. Suddenly it popped free! And then I was floating in the air! Bobbing up against the ceiling!

Chapter 2

"Spencer!" I yelled. "I'm on the ceiling!"

I peered down. I could see my own body. It was still lying on my bed. My eyes were closed. My left hand was still on my forehead. My right hand was still over my belly button.

Weird! I was seeing myself the way other people see me.

There was Spencer, lying on the top bunk. His eyes were closed. He wasn't moving. Was he sleeping, or what?

"Hey, Spencer!" I called. "Are you in there?"

"No!" said a voice right behind me. "I'm out here!"

I turned my head.

Spencer was bobbing against the ceiling right next to me! He looked about the same. Only you could sort of see through him. And he looked kind of sparkly.

"We did it!" I said. "We actually got out of our bodies!"

"Of course," said Spencer. Just like he did it every night of his life.

This was amazing. My body felt lighter than air. My body felt like it had no weight. My body felt like I had no body.

Moving around was fun. I found out that if I breathed out, I started to sink. But if I breathed in, I rose. To go forward, all I had to do was move my arms and legs, like I was swimming. Swimming in the air. Just for the fun of it, I did a loop-the-loop.

"This is very cool," I said.

"So where would you like to travel to?" Spencer asked.

"I don't know," I said. "Where could we go?"

"Anywhere we want," said Spencer. He had a big sparkling grin on his face.

"How about into my dad's study?" I said.

"I was thinking more like Egypt," said Spencer.

Spencer had just done a geography project on Egypt. He built a pyramid out of 743 sugar cubes. It was pretty amazing.

"What would we do in Egypt?" I asked.

"I don't know," said Spencer. "Go down the Nile. See the pyramids."

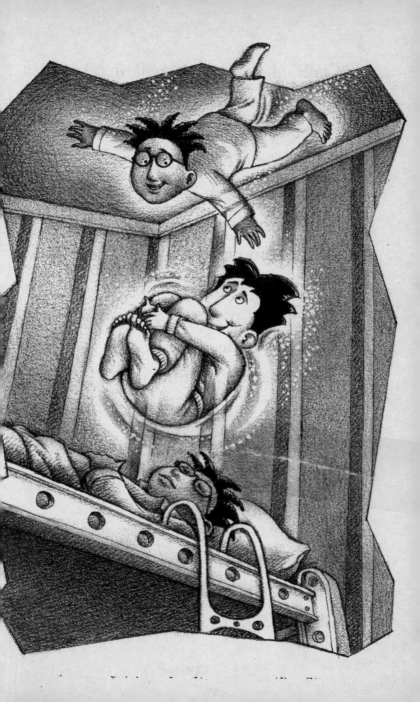

"Cool!" I said. "But will it take us a long time to get there?"

"Probably," said Spencer. "Egypt is more than 5,000 miles away."

"Well, we have to be back by morning," I said. "Otherwise my dad will worry. Let's pick something closer to home. How about the Bronx Zoo?"

"The zoo is fine," said Spencer.

I floated to the door. It was closed. I couldn't open it. I couldn't even grip the doorknob. I floated to the window. It was closed too.

"How are we ever going to get out of here?" I asked.

"What if you go through the wall?" said Spencer.

"And just how do I do that?" I asked.

"Like this," said Spencer.

He put his hands together over his head. He did a scissors kick with his legs. He dove into my bedroom wall. His hands disappeared. Then his head. Then the rest of him. Spencer slid through the wall like it was Jell-O.

Awesome!

"Hey! Wait for me!" I called out.

I put my hands together and pushed off. My head went through the wall. I saw flashes of wood and brick. I felt nothing.

And then I was outside.

Yikes!

I was thirty stories up!

There was nothing underneath me but air! Far below me were the tiny lights of the city.

Help!

Chapter 3

I panicked. The air rushed out of my lungs. I began to fall. Then I remembered to breathe in. And I floated back up. Spencer was waiting for me, giggling.

"So, are we going to the zoo?" he asked.

"Follow me," I said.

We left Dad's building on East 52nd Street. We flew uptown...over the tops of tall buildings...over Park Avenue...over lines of cars going both ways...and then over Central Park. I felt like Superman. I could almost hear the music from the *Superman* movies.

"Is this great, or what?" Spencer shouted.

"The greatest!" I shouted back.

Soon we were flying over the Bronx Zoo.

"Ladies and gentlemen," I said, "this is your captain. We are about to land at the Bronx Zoo. Please make sure that your seat belts are securely fastened. And your seat backs and tray tables must be in the upright and locked position."

We floated down toward the ground.

"Ladies and gentlemen," I went on, "we have arrived at the Bronx Zoo. We hope you have a pleasant evening. We thank you for flying Out-of-Body Airlines. For those of you in our Frequent Flier program, tonight's flight is worth fifteen miles."

The zoo was closed. There were no people—except for Spencer and me. But, come to think of it, I'm not sure we really counted as people. It was very dark. And far away you could hear a wolf or something howling.

"It's a lot creepier here at night," said Spencer.

I nodded. "But as long as we're here, let's go see the lions," I said. I'm crazy about lions.

We went to the lion area. We didn't see any lions.

"So, where are they?" I asked.

"In bed, I bet," said Spencer. "It's night-time."

"Then they must be right inside that cave," I said. "Let's go and have a look."

"Zack, are you crazy?"

"Spencer, we're out of our bodies."

"And you're out of your mind."

"But if we're not in our bodies," I said, "they can't hurt us. Right?"

Spencer seemed to see the logic of that.

"C'mon!" I said.

We floated into the cave. You couldn't see a thing. But you could hear the snoring. It was a weird sound. A bunch of huge pussycats, snoring in the dark. Then one of them coughed. OK, it was half a cough and half a roar.

"Zack," Spencer whispered right near me, "this is a really dumb idea."

"Why?"

"Why? Because. They might wake up. And they might just decide to bite our astral butts off."

"Hmmmm. Maybe you've got a point there," I said.

With me leading the way, we floated back toward the cave entrance.

Our astral eyes must have gotten used to the dark. Or maybe it was just brighter at the cave entrance. Because when we got there, we didn't have any trouble seeing the huge lion that was standing in front of us.

It was the biggest lion I had ever seen. Or maybe I'd just never seen a lion up close before.

"M-maybe he c-can't see us," Spencer whispered.

I raised my hand and waved it a little.

The lion didn't seem to notice. I waved both my arms. The lion opened his mouth. And yawned.

"He *can't* see us!" I said.

So I moved toward the lion.

Weird! Now the lion took a step backward.

I went a little nearer. The lion moved back farther.

"Wow! He senses we're here," Spencer whispered.

"And *he's* afraid of *us*!" I said out loud.

The lion took a step forward. And roared.

"OK," I said, "so he's not afraid of us."

"We should get out of here," Spencer whispered.

"Spencer," I said, "follow me!"

I backed up several feet. I put my hands

together and dove toward an open space at the lion's right.

Oops! The lion moved to the right. And opened his mouth. Wide.

I tried to stop. I couldn't. I dove straight into the lion's mouth, with Spencer right behind me.

Chapter 4

We went through the lion's mouth. We slid right through his body. We were free!

A second later we were zooming up and away from the Bronx Zoo.

"Where are we going now?" Spencer called.

"You'll see!" I said.

The amusement park at Coney Island in Brooklyn was as dark and deserted as the zoo. The humps of roller-coaster hills looked like dinosaur skeletons. It was cool, in a very weird way.

Spencer wanted to go on the roller coaster right away. Of course, the cars weren't running. So we decided to go on it *without* the cars. Going down the hills headfirst was really fun. But unless you're out of your body, I don't suggest you try it.

Our next stop was the Statue of Liberty. I've always wanted to go to the very top. But I never felt like standing in line or climbing up all those stairs. Spencer and I flew to the top of the torch. It was an awesome view.

Then I got an idea. I flew right under the Statue of Liberty's nose.

"Guess what I am!" I yelled to Spencer.

"I give up."

"An astral booger!"

After that we headed uptown again. On Broadway near Times Square, we saw a long line stretching around the block.

Terminator 3000 had just opened. None of our parents wanted us to see it. About a million people get killed in all kinds of horrible ways.

"Now's our chance!" said Spencer.

So down we flew. We went right through all the people in line. And, of course, we didn't have to pay!

The popcorn smelled great. I went over to help myself to a bag. But then it hit me. I couldn't eat any. Bummer!

Spencer was looking at a bunch of video games in the lobby. There were lots of cool ones. But every time we tried to hold on to

the controls, our astral hands just slipped right through them.

So we waited for the movie to begin. Usually I get stuck behind some guy who's about seven feet tall. This time, no problem. Spencer and I had a perfect view from up near the ceiling.

The trouble was, the movie was way scarier than we thought it would be. I looked at Spencer. He looked at me.

"I think we ought to go back home now," I said.

"Why?" said Spencer.

"Because," I said. "I need my sleep. If I don't get home and get some sleep, I'm going to be a mess tomorrow."

"You *are* home asleep," said Spencer. "At least your body is. The rest of you can stay out as late as you like."

"I still think we ought to go home," I said.

"Uh, OK," said Spencer.

Little did I know the scariest part of our adventure was waiting for us there!

Chapter 5

By the time we got back to my dad's apartment and slid through the wall into my room, it was really late. I wanted to go to bed. Even though I didn't have to. Weird, huh?

"OK, Spencer," I said, "how do we get back into our bodies?"

"There are several ways to do that," he said.

"Which one should we use?"

"Uh, probably the one the book says."

"And what does the book say?"

"Well, let's see here."

He floated over to the book, which was beside his body on the top bunk.

"Well?" I said.

"There seems to be a little problem," he said.

"What kind of a little problem?"

"The book is opened to page thirteen," he said. "That's the page for getting out of our bodies. The directions for getting back *in* are on the next page. On page fourteen."

"Well, turn the page."

Spencer looked at me.

"Oh, no," I said. I smacked my astral forehead with my astral hand. "You can't turn the page."

"I could if I were in my body," he said.

"If you were in your body, you wouldn't *have* to," I said.

"Right."

"What do we do if we can't get back into our bodies?" I said.

Spencer shrugged nervously. That spooked me. Spencer always knows the answer to any question. But not this time.

"Maybe Dad can help us," I said.

I swam through my bedroom door and floated into Dad's bedroom. Spencer followed me.

Dad was fast asleep. One leg was hanging down off the bed. His eyes were closed. His mouth was open. And he was kind of drooling onto his pillow.

"Dad!" I yelled. "Wake up!"

He went on sleeping.

I floated down to his head. I put my lips right up to his ear.

"Dad! Wake up! We're in trouble!"

Dad is a very sound sleeper. He didn't move an inch.

"Spencer," I said, "Dad is not waking up."

"I can see that," said Spencer. He was floating right beside me. He thought for a moment. Then he said, "What if we go to Mrs. Coleman-Levin's house?"

"What good would that do?" I asked.

Mrs. Coleman-Levin is our science and homeroom teacher. She's also kind of weird. She keeps a pig's brain in a jar on her desk. She wears work boots, even for dressy parties. And on weekends she does autopsies at the morgue. That means she cuts up dead bodies to see what they died of. Ugh!

"She knows about lots of weird stuff," said Spencer. "Maybe she can help. And I happen to know she stays up till dawn."

I didn't have a better idea. So I said, "Why not?"

Spencer knew the way to Mrs. Coleman-Levin's house. He got extra credit one vacation for catching live insects to feed to her huge Venus fly trap. He led the way across town to her apartment.

Mrs. Coleman-Levin's apartment was very cool. It looked like a rain forest. It had a huge palm tree and lots of tropical plants and hanging vines and stuff like that. It even had a little waterfall. And, of course, the Venus fly trap.

We found Mrs. Coleman-Levin's room. She was in bed. Fast asleep. With her work boots on.

"Spencer, I thought you said she stays up till dawn," I said. "It isn't dawn yet."

"Then I was wrong," said Spencer.

"Or else she's still up," said another voice.

The voice had come from above. We looked up.

Mrs. Coleman-Levin was sitting cross-legged near the ceiling!

Chapter 6

"Mrs. Coleman-Levin! You're out of your body!" I shouted.

"A splendid observation, Zack," she said.

"But how did you do that?" asked Spencer.

"How did *you*?" she said.

"We learned from a book," I said.

"Good place to learn," she said. "Where have you gone since you've been out?"

"To the Bronx Zoo," I said. "And Coney

Island. And the Statue of Liberty. And the movies."

"Sounds like you've had a pretty full night," she said.

"We have," said Spencer.

"Why did you come to see me?"

"We don't know how to get back into our bodies," Spencer said. "We thought you might know."

"I *do* know," she said.

"Great!" I said. "Will you tell us?"

"Of course not," she said with a smile.

"Why not?" I said.

"Because. If I tell you, you won't learn anything. If you figure it out for yourself, you will."

"We could find out from the book," said Spencer. "But the book is opened to page thirteen. And the directions for getting

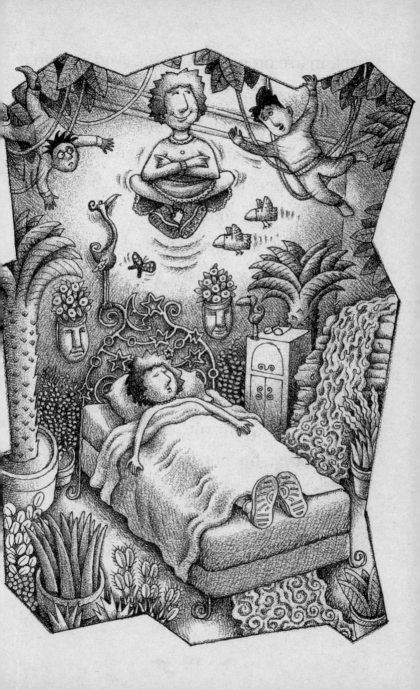

back in are on page fourteen. And we can't turn the page."

"Then I suggest you do some experimenting," she said. Mrs. Coleman-Levin is big on experimenting. "And I bet you'll come up with a solution."

Mrs. Coleman-Levin waved good-bye. I guess we were supposed to leave.

"Won't you tell us anything at all?" I asked.

"Why, certainly," she said. "I'll tell you that no one who's in his or her body can see you. Or hear you. But you both are smart boys. So put your astral minds to work. Because if you're not inside your bodies and in class promptly at 8:30 on Monday morning, I'm going to have to mark you absent. And I would hate to do that!"

Chapter 7

By the time we got back to Dad's apart-ment, it was Sunday morning. Both Spencer and I were tired of being out of our bodies. As much fun as it is passing through walls and flying over the city, it's nice to be able to scratch your neck. Or snuggle down in bed. Or eat a bagel and cream cheese for breakfast. I never thought I'd miss simple stuff like that.

We swam into my room. There we

were—on the top and bottom bunks. Just where we left us.

"What do we do now?" I asked.

"I don't know," said Spencer. "Why don't you try climbing into your body through your mouth?"

I floated over to my body.

"My mouth is closed," I said.

"Well, *that's* unusual," said Spencer.

I glared at him.

Spencer floated up to his body and looked at it.

"Mine is closed too," he said. "Hey, why don't you try to fit yourself in through your nostril?"

I looked at my body and shook my head.

"I couldn't fit more than a finger in there," I said.

"I've already seen you do that," said Spencer.

I gave him a punch on his astral arm. It passed right through his arm and out the other side.

Suddenly something small and furry scampered across the top bunk. Then it ran down the wall and stopped on the bottom bunk.

"Yikes!" I said. "It's the mouse!"

"You're afraid of a *mouse*?" said Spencer. "You're a guy who dove into a lion's mouth."

"It just surprised me, that's all," I said. "Spencer, what if we can't figure out how to get back into our bodies?"

"Then Monday morning Mrs. Coleman-Levin will mark us absent," said Spencer.

"Never mind Mrs. Coleman-Levin," I said. "In an hour or so, my dad's going to come in here to wake us for breakfast. If he can't wake us, what's he going to think?"

"That we're unconscious," said Spencer.

I nodded. Dad was not going to react well to that.

"We've got to figure something out," I said. "Spencer, you're the genius. Think of something!"

"Hmmmm. Maybe we should try the Scientific Method," Spencer suggested. The Scientific Method is something else Mrs. Coleman-Levin is always talking about. It's the way real scientists solve problems.

"We might as well," I said.

"Step one in the Scientific Method is to observe," said Spencer. "Well, I observe that there's no way we can turn the page on that book ourselves."

So far I was with him.

"Step two is to form a theory," Spencer went on.

"OK," I said.

"I have a theory that we could get some-body to turn that page for us," said Spencer.

"And who, exactly, did you have in mind?" I said.

Just then the mouse reappeared from under my bed. It scampered across the rug.

"The mouse, of course," said Spencer.

"The mouse?" I said.

Spencer saw I looked doubtful.

"Zack, animals can't see us," he said. "But the lion did seem to sense us."

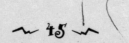

"True," I said. "But so what?"

"Well," said Spencer, "maybe we can corner the mouse by the book. Maybe we can get him to run across the page and turn it over."

Hmmmm. Well, it was a long shot. But for now it was all we had.

"OK," I said. "Let's go for it."

"Step three: Test the theory," said Spencer.

So we did. The mouse was starting to nibble on my teddy bear. I didn't like that at all. I floated toward my teddy bear. The mouse looked up.

"Hi, mouse," I said. I don't know why I was talking to a mouse, but I was. "You can't see us, but we're here. We're boys. Boys who like mice. We need you to do us a favor. Just go up to the top bunk. And

run across that book. And turn the page for us."

The mouse seemed confused. He seemed spooked. He backed away from me.

Good! He was moving in the right direction. He ran up to the top bunk. Toward the book. But then he ran past the book and down the wall to the floor. And then he disappeared.

"Darn!" I said.

"So much for the Scientific Method," said Spencer.

Just then my bedroom door opened. Dad stuck his head in. He looked toward the bunk beds.

Boy, was I glad to see him!

"Dad!" I shouted, forgetting he couldn't hear us. "We're in trouble! We really need your help!"

"Aw, they look so cute asleep," said my dad.

"No, Dad! We're not asleep! We're not cute! We're up here!" I shouted.

"Good morning, gentlemen," said my dad. "Who'd like waffles with strawberry jam for breakfast?"

"Dad!" I said. "You have *got* to help us!"

Dad walked over to the bed. He gently shook my body by the shoulders.

"Wake up, Zack," he said.

"Dad! I'm not asleep! I'm just not inside my body!"

"Zack?"

Dad looked puzzled.

"Dad! How can I get through to you?"

"Zack, what's wrong with you? Are you faking?"

Dad stood up and poked Spencer. Then

Dad saw the book. The out-of-body book. He picked it up and looked at it.

"What the...? *Astral Travel for Beginners*?"

"Yes! That's right! He's going to figure it out, Spencer! My dad is going to figure it out!"

Dad took a fast peek inside the book.

"Hmmmm," he said. "Did you guys find a way to leave your bodies?"

"We did!" I screamed. "Yes! That's exactly what we did!"

"If you'd left your bodies," said my dad, "you'd probably be invisible...."

"Yes, Dad! Yes!" I screamed. "We are!"

"You might even be floating right in front of my face. And I couldn't see you...."

"Yes!" I screamed. "That's right!"

"You might even be talking to me. And I couldn't even hear you...."

"We are, Dad! We are!"

"Hi, Zack," said my dad. But he was facing the wrong direction. He was talking to the air. Then he shook his head.

"Nah!" he said. "These guys probably stayed up till dawn, talking. I'll just let them sleep some more. I'll come back in a few minutes."

Dad tossed the book on the floor and walked to the door.

"No, Dad! Don't leave!"

The door closed behind Dad.

"Well," I said, "at least he'll be back in a few minutes."

"Yes," said Spencer. "And when we still don't wake up, he's going to freak."

That was true. Poor Dad. He'd think we were both in a coma or something.

"Spencer, what are we going to do?"

Spencer didn't answer me. He was staring at the book.

"Zack!" shouted Spencer. "Look!"

"What?"

"Page fourteen," he said. "When your dad threw the book down, the page turned. I can just make out the directions."

"Let me see," I said.

"Better yet," he said, "I'll read them to you. Do exactly as I say!"

"OK," I said.

"First," said Spencer, reading aloud, "did you have a totally groovy time out of your body? Did you feel totally at one with the universe? Are you ready now to re-enter your body?"

"Yes!" I shouted.

"Then get parallel with your body," Spencer continued. "Float just a few inches above it...."

"OK," I said.

I floated over to the lower bunk. I got parallel with my body. I floated a few inches above it.

"Make sure the hands of your astral body are in the same place as those of your real body," Spencer read. "Your left hand on your forehead, over your third eye. Your right hand on your navel..."

"OK," I said.

"Listen to your wind chimes," he read.

"Forget the wind chimes!" I said.

"Now, close your eyes and picture a big funnel in your navel...." he continued.

"OK," I said.

"Pour yourself through that funnel," Spencer read, "right into your navel. Just like a bucket of sand."

"OK," I said.

I closed my eyes. I pictured the funnel. I pictured pouring myself into it like a bucket of sand.

Whoosh! In I went!

I felt my body start to come alive again! Parts of me began to tingle. First my toes and fingers. Then my wrists and ankles. Then my legs and arms. Then my chest and lungs. And finally my head and face.

I opened up my eyes. I was back in my body!

"I'm back in!" I shouted.

I looked around for Spencer. He was gone.

"Spencer!" I called. "Where are you?"

And then I realized: I was back in my body. I could no longer see anybody who was out of theirs.

I climbed the ladder to the top bunk.

Spencer looked like he was fast asleep. If he wasn't back in his body, then where was he?

"Spencer!" I shouted. "Speak to me!"

Suddenly Spencer's eyes snapped open.

"What do you want me to say?" said Spencer.

I giggled. Just then Dad came back into my bedroom.

"Well, well, well, you're finally awake," he said. "What time did you guys get to sleep?"

Spencer and I looked at each other.

"It's a long story, sir," said Spencer.

"Then tell me," said my dad. "I'm a writer. I love long stories."

So we all went in to breakfast. Let me tell you. Waffles with strawberry jam had never tasted so good!

That night Dad didn't have to nag me about going to bed. I wanted to get to school early on Monday.

I couldn't wait for Mrs. Coleman-Levin to see Spencer and me.

No way was she going to mark us absent!

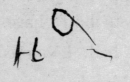